To:
Bella
+ Gianna
From: Crazy
Uncle Bones + Auntie
Sarah
Merry Christmas!

Who sat on me?

with Polly the porcupine

created and illustrated by
Jacqui Brown

One warm afternoon,
Polly the porcupine
was asleep in the sun.

Suddenly, someone sat down
right on top of poor Polly!

"OUCH!" she cried.
"Who sat on me?"

Polly opened her eyes and
saw a huge, gray bottom
disappearing into the trees.

Who did it belong to?
Polly decided to find out.

The first bottom
that Polly found
was not the right one.
It was too stripy.

But who did it belong to?

The bottom belonged to
Zara the zebra.

Zara's favorite game
was hide and seek.

The next bottom
that Polly found
was the wrong color.

But who did it belong to?

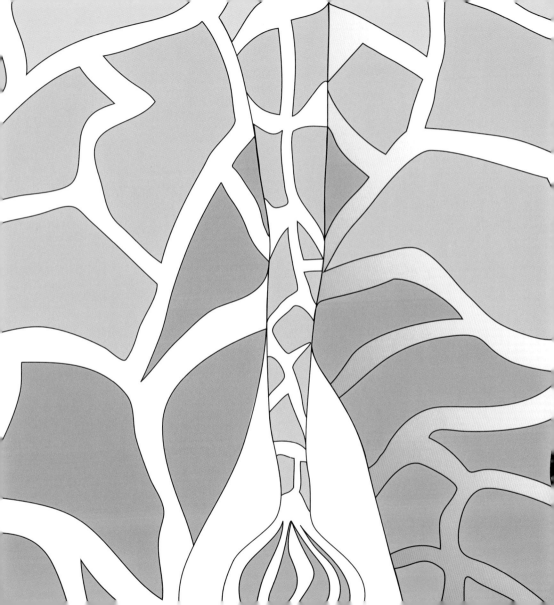

It belonged to
Gustav the giraffe.

He had a head for heights.

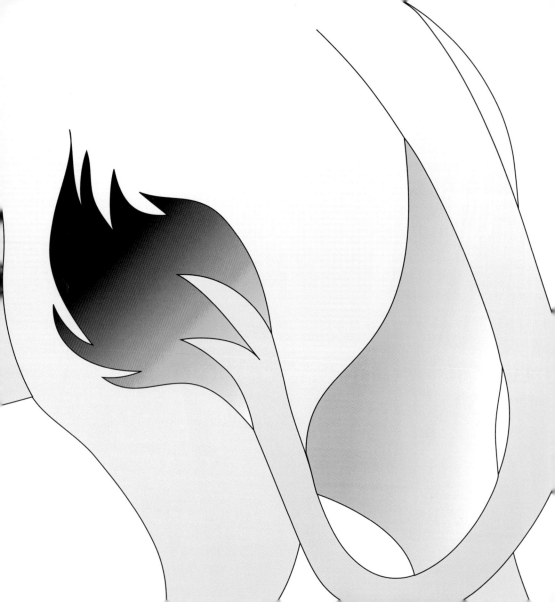

The third bottom
that Polly found
was too furry.

But who did it belong to?

It belonged to Leo the lion.

He sometimes got very cross.

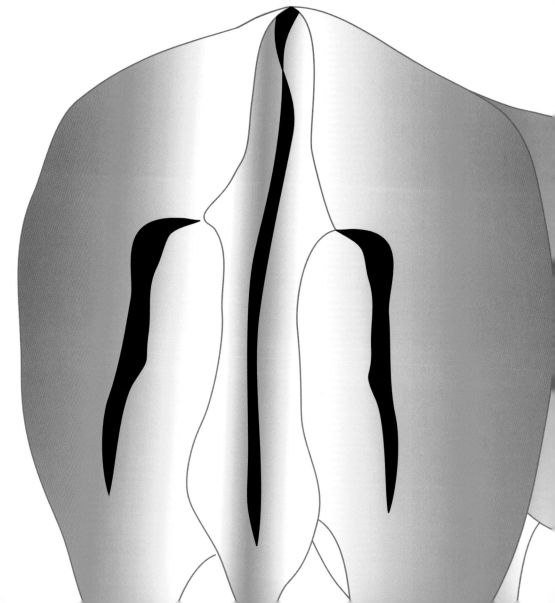

The next bottom
that Polly found
was too thin.

But who did it belong to?

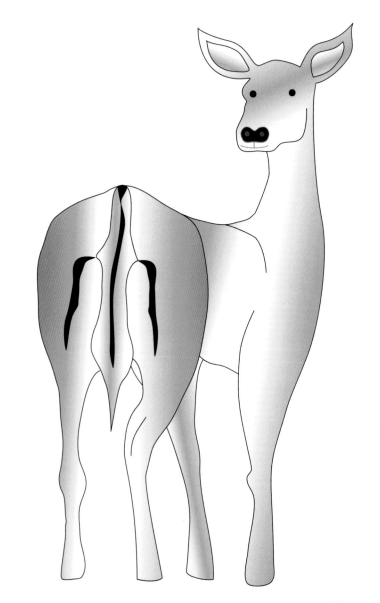

It belonged to
Annie the antelope.

She liked to jump around a lot.

The next bottom
that Polly saw
was definitely not
the right one.
It was full of feathers.

But who did
it belong to?

It belonged to
Oliver the ostrich.

He was better
at running than flying.

At last Polly saw
a huge, gray bottom.
It was full of quills.

"This is the bottom
I've been looking for,"
said Polly.

Who do you think
it belonged to?

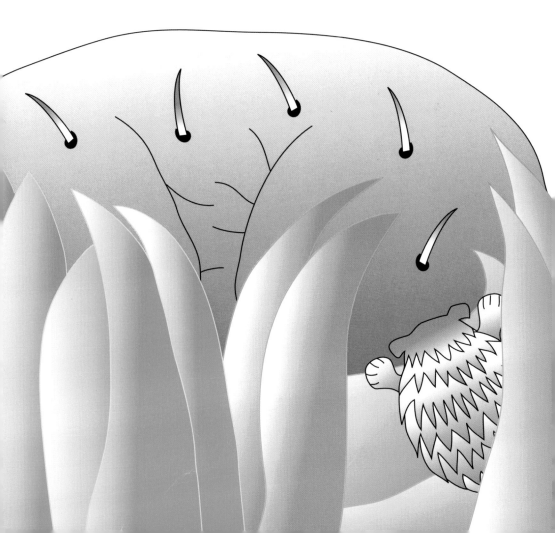

The huge, gray bottom
belonged to
Ellie the elephant.

"I'm sorry
I sat on you,"
said Ellie.
"I didn't see you."

Polly's sharp quills
were stuck in
Ellie's bottom, and
they HURT!

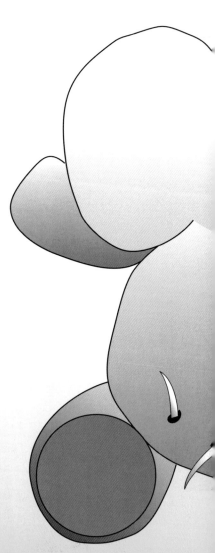

Polly helped Ellie
pull out
all the quills.

Polly would be more careful
where she slept in the future.
And Ellie would be
much more careful
where she sat!